To Benny + Sammy
+ Danny,

I hope you grow
up to love reading
as much as I do!

Love,
Hepburn

D1172277

Hepburn
The Downtown Dog

Written by Amanda Drewry
Illustrated by Morgan Cash
Edited by Mary Lou Mathews

Printed in the United States of America

ISBN 978-0-9974391-0-6
Library of Congress Control Number 2016937076

Hepburn the Downtown Dog, LLC
2817 West End Avenue, #129-196
Nashville, TN 37203

www.hepburnthedowntowndog.com

Special thank you to:

Connell Memorial United Methodist Church
Goodlettsville, TN

H. B. Williams Elementary School
White House, TN

Stephanie Hall and Chad Ray

B.J. Drewry, Joann Drewry, Brenda Cash, Reba Adams

And to all of our supportive friends and family!

Hello, my name is Hepburn,
I would like to be your friend!
I have a story for you.
I hope you will stay till the end!

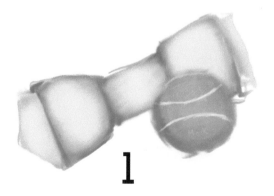

1

I once was a small puppy
Born way out in the country,
Awaiting my adoption
By someone who would love me.

Way back in my puppy days,
I wanted friends on the farm.
I tried making friends with chickens,
But they thought I would cause them harm.

I tried making friends with cows,
But they thought I was too small.
They said I was too fluffy,
And I did not fit in at all.

I tried making friends with pigs,
But they said I was too groomed.
When I tried to join their mud pit,
They said there was no room.

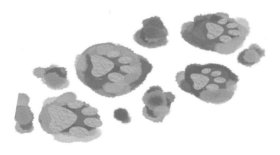

I was sad until one day
A car came down the road.
I wondered who was in it
And just where we would go.

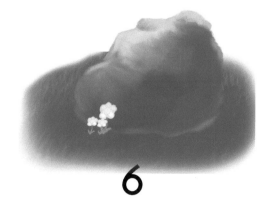

Out popped Miss Amanda,
And she was my new mom!
She was taking me to Nashville
To be a downtown dog!

Right then I coined my phrase.
I would bark, "Hep Hep Hooray!"
When something splendid happens,
Just like it did that day!

Hep Hep Hooray!

We arrived in the city,
And I got to see downtown.
My tail just wagged and wagged
To see the buildings all around.

9

With my head out of the window
And my ears flopping in the breeze,
I loved the sounds I heard
In Nashville, Tennessee!

I heard roars of a crowd
Cheering at a football game.
I heard sounds of country music
When we passed a hall of fame!

I saw beautiful, big buildings,
Made of glass, concrete and stone.
There was one shaped like a bat,
And one was my new home!

When we entered the large lobby,
There sat a red-haired man.
He said his name was Lance,
And then my tour began!

Lance

13

"He is our friend and concierge,"
Miss Amanda said to me.
"Whenever we need help,
There our buddy Lance will be."

'CON-SEE-ERZH'
14

Lance

Concierge

When we reached the elevator,
Lance saw that I hesitated.
He told me not to worry
And sang a song while we waited!

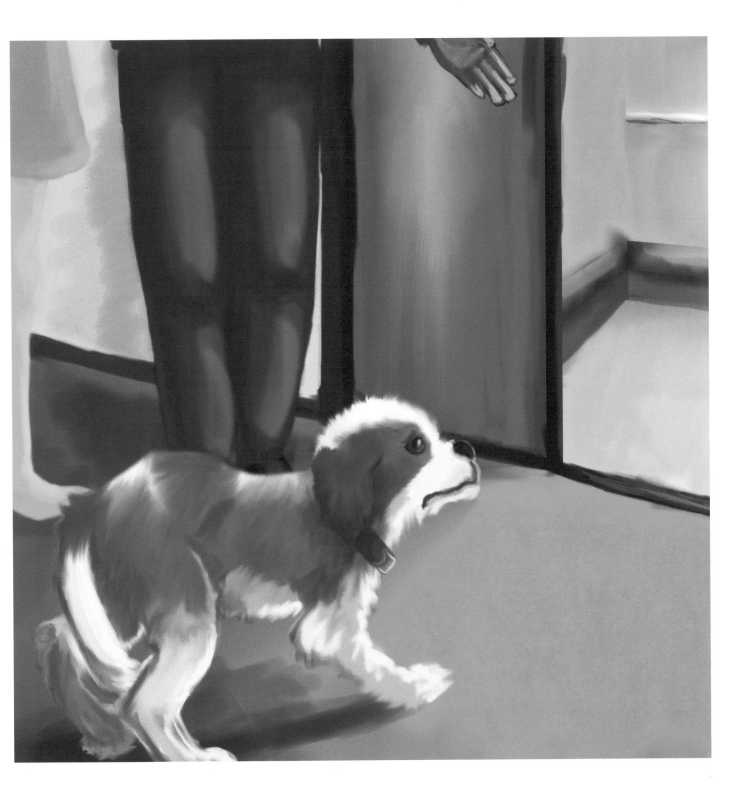

"Elevator, elevator!
Ride the floors up and down!
Elevator, elevator!
Ride until we touch the ground!"

The elevator opened
To a giant rooftop pool!
I could see myself in it
Wearing shades and looking cool!

17

Next she took me to our condo.
I saw my bowl, my toys and bone.
She had my new bed waiting,
And I felt loved instead of alone.

I barked, "Hep Hep Hooray!"
As I licked Miss Amanda's face.
I was glad she was my mom,
And this was my forever place.

Hep Hep Hooray!

I knew I was somewhere
That I finally fit in.
I was now a Downtown Dog,
And my adventures would begin!

Hepburn

Hepburn's Prayer:

"Let's bow our paws
and say our thanks.
For bones, friends, treats and grace.
Thank you GOD
for all you've done!
Being a dog is so much fun!!"

CPSIA information can be obtained
at www.ICGtesting.com
Printed in the USA
LVHW072045120419
614049LV00001B/1/P